First published in 2001
by Hodder Children's Books
This paperback edition published in 2007

Hodder Children's Books
338 Euston Road, London NW1 3BH

Hodder Children's Books Australia
Level 17/207 Kent Street, Sydney, NSW 2000

A catalogue record of this book is
available from the British Library.

ISBN: 978 0 340 81804 6

Printed in China

Hodder Children's Books is a
division of Hachette Children's Books.

Kipper and Roly

Mick Inkpen

Hodder
Children's
Books

A division of Hachette Children's Books

Pig was writing the invitations to his birthday party.
This was his present list.

1. A pet. Like a rabbit, or a guinea pig, or something.
2. A little mouse or a gerbil.
3. Anything else.
   (But mostly I would like Number 1, or Number 2.)

He put the names on the envelopes and wondered what kind of pet he would get.

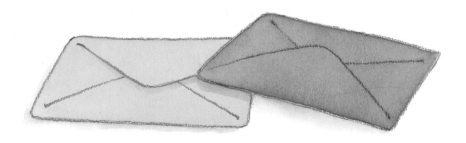

When Kipper's invitation arrived, he read it and rushed off to the pet shop to choose a pet for Pig.

The rabbit? Too sleepy.

The guinea pigs? Too timid.

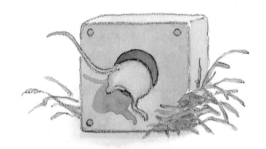

The mouse? Too shy.

The stick insect? Too much like a stick. Boring.

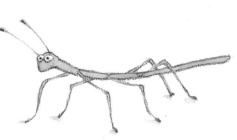

But the hamster? The hamster was not sleepy, nor timid, nor shy, and it wasn't like a stick at all!

It was perfect.

'One of these please!' said Kipper.

At home Kipper gave the
hamster some sunflower seeds.
It stuffed them into its cheeks.

'Are you always this hungry?'
said Kipper. The hamster ran up
Kipper's arm and sat on his shoulder,
cleaning its whiskers. Then it ran
down the other arm and rolled
across the table.

'You can do a roly poly!'
said Kipper.
'You're so clever!'
The hamster
did it again.

T he morning of the
party, Roly Poly
woke Kipper by
nibbling on his ear.
        'I wish I didn't have
to give you to Pig today,' said Kipper.
        At breakfast Kipper began to think
that maybe he would keep Roly and
buy a rabbit for Pig instead.
        'No. He'd like you better,'
sighed Kipper. 'Come on.
Let's wrap up your cage.'

Kipper got out some scissors and some sticky tape, and unrolled a roll of wrapping paper.

Roly ran into the cardboard tube and popped out at the other end, making Kipper giggle. Then he slid all the way down the tube and rolled across the floor, making Kipper giggle again.

It gave Kipper an idea.

A big idea.

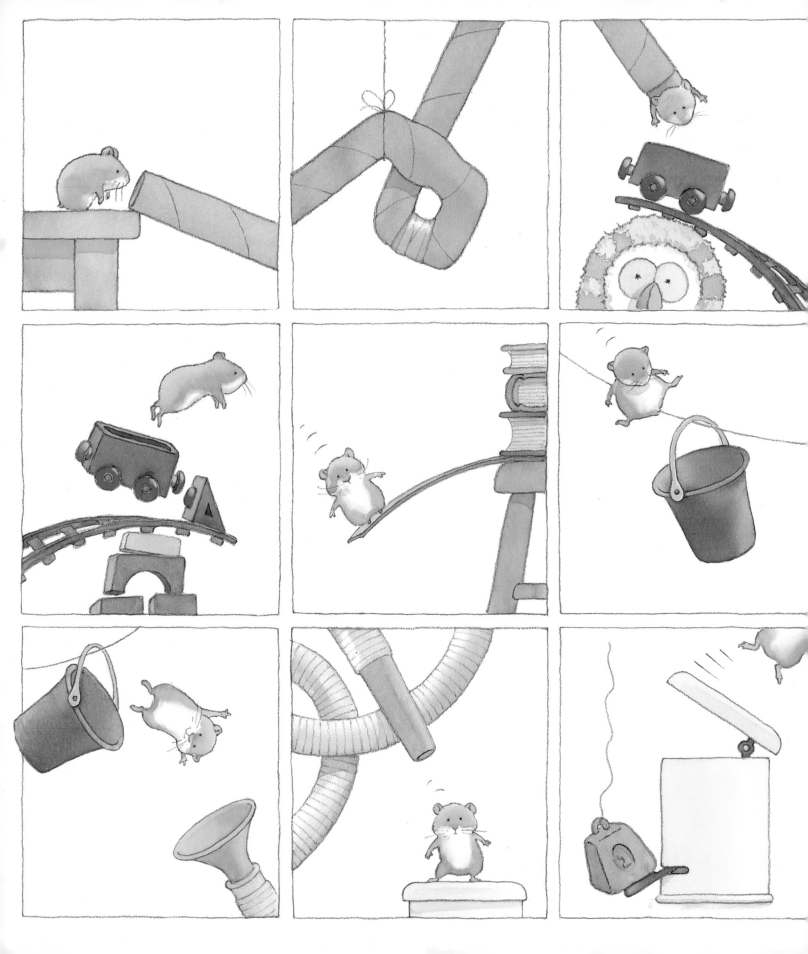

This was Kipper's big idea. It took him ages. But it worked perfectly!

'You're the best birthday present ever!' said Kipper, as Roly dropped into his paws. It was then that he remembered Pig's party!

Kipper rushed off to Pig's house. Halfway there he met Jake and Tiger, coming the other way.

'Where were you?' said Tiger. 'The party's over!' But Kipper wasn't listening. He was thinking about Roly Poly.

'I can't stop!' he said. 'I don't think he likes it in there very much.'

Jake and Tiger began to giggle.

'Oh, no! Not another one!' said Tiger.

'I'm sorry I'm late!' said Kipper
to Pig, as he opened the door.
'I was playing with
your present!
He's brilliant,
isn't he?'

Then he noticed that Pig was
holding a rabbit, a mouse and two
guinea pigs, and there was a
stick insect crawling across his head.
'What are those?' said Kipper.
'They're my presents,' said Pig.

They sat down at Pig's table and Kipper fed Roly with pieces of left-over party cake.

'So he's not really what you wanted?' said Kipper.

'He's exactly what I wanted,' said Pig, 'before I had all these.'

He pointed at his other pets. 'But it's my own fault. I should have thought of something else to put on my present list.'

Kipper took a big bite of cake for himself.

'He's very nice though, isn't he?' said Kipper. 'His name is Roly Poly. Because he can do roly polies. He's really good at them! And he's always hungry. He keeps his food in his cheeks! Look!'

Pig looked at Roly's little, fat face. It was his turn to have an idea.

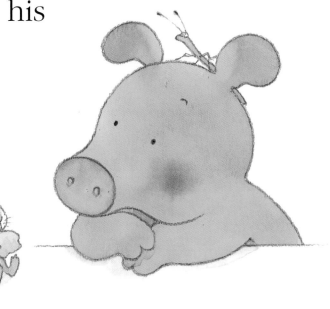

'Kipper,' said Pig, 'would you do me a favour? Would you look after him for me?'

Kipper was so surprised he almost choked on his cake.

'What? Take him home, you mean?' said Kipper.

Pig nodded.

'You mean he'd still be yours, but I'd look after him?'

Pig nodded again.

'OH, YES!'

said Kipper.

He said it so loudly, that all of Pig's pets jumped off the table and hid underneath.

Kipper picked up Roly Poly, sat him back down and fed him another piece of cake. Roly Poly stopped eating for a second, hiccuped . . .

. . .and started eating again.